I0518128

Groatcrest
By James Field

ISBN 978-0-9957166-8-1

First Edition

Dedicated to all those people who have suffered brain damage as a consequence of electroconvulsive 'therapy'.

Adele

My husband Ralph is rubbing his forefinger and thumb together again. I think he does it absent-mindedly. It always reminds me of a housefly rubbing its forelimbs together. I know flies do it to clean themselves, but it always looks so unpleasantly covetous to me.

I'm sitting alongside Ralph at home on our sofa in the sitting room. He's showing me his photo album, which contains photos depicting his life both before and after he met me. We married a year after we met, and we've been married for just six months, so we haven't known each other for all that long.

'Hey Adele, look at this one,' he says.

I gaze at the picture. It shows Ralph looking younger, and he's dancing with a very pretty woman, who's wearing a stylish red dress and a radiant smile. She is leaning backwards gracefully and being supported in his outstretched arms.

'That's Letitia, an absolute beauty I met in Paris about ten years ago,' he says with unmistakable wistfulness.

'Ralph, please...' I murmur.

'Now contrast how sublime that is to this one I took of you last week,' he says, ignoring my protest and pointing at a photograph in which I'm dancing listlessly, resembling somebody who looks glum and alone.

He turns a page of the album and points at a photo of another woman. 'Oh, now this one brings back memories!' he cries admiringly. 'That's Sophia. Lovely Sophia, who is unsurpassed in gorgeousness, poise and elegance!'

I peer at it with grudging curiosity. I see a very attractive woman with a glowing complexion in a seated position, grinning coquettishly at the camera. Ralph is standing close behind her, one hand resting on her delicate shoulder.

'Look at her excellent posture and dignity,' Ralph gushes. Then he flicks over a page and jabs his finger at a photo of me that I remember he took last week. I'm sitting down and looking glumly at the camera. 'And now, contrast her with this one of you, looking like a sour trout with your shoulders sagging all over the shop,' he says in tones of measured bitterness.

'Ralph that's enough now!' I say, pushing the album away. 'I don't want to see any more!'

Ralph is always showing me pictures of the women from his past and comparing me unfavourably. It never fails to make me feel utterly belittled.

'Alright, don't be such a drama queen! They're only photographs. Keep your hair on.'

Before long, Ralph tells me he'd like us to go for a drive.

'Where are we going?' I ask.

'We're just going for a spin, that's all.'

I comb my hair, put on some lippy, and check that I've got everything I might need in my handbag. Then I'm ready to go.

Once we're both settled in the car, Ralph behind the wheel, he flashes me the briefest of sidelong glances. There's something cold in it, I'm sure of it. Then he turns the key in the ignition and eases the vehicle off the drive.

I move to put the radio on, but he switches it off immediately. He shakes his head, saying, 'I'd rather just have a bit of peace and quiet if you don't mind, love.'

We've only been travelling for around five minutes when Ralph parks the car. We're still in a residential area, not so many streets away from our own house. He makes no movement to get out of the car. He doesn't unclip his seatbelt and leaves the engine running. He just settles into his seat and sits staring out of the window on my passenger side. I follow his gaze out to a house with a well-tended garden, full of the inviting colours of spring.

Maybe one of Ralph's friends lives here, I surmise.

We sit in the car in silence. I'm waiting for him to turn the engine off or say something, but he just stays sitting and gazing at the house.

'So, what are we doing then, Ralph?' I say. 'Are we here as guests for dinner? I wish you'd have told me, so I could have worn something a bit dressier.'

He doesn't reply and just keeps gazing.

'Ralph, what on earth's the matter?'

Still he says nothing. He doesn't look at me once.

Minutes pass by.

'Earth calling Ralph,' I say, waving my hand in front of his face in what I hope is a comical manner.

He flaps my hand away. 'Just keep watching,' he says.

Five more minutes pass by, and I'm starting to feel quite restless. In these moments of idleness, it occurs to me that there are wildlife enthusiasts who are capable of sitting for hours, patiently waiting for a glimpse of some rare creature. You've got to respect that. But at least they have the advantage of knowing what they're waiting for.

Around fifteen more minutes pass. Then I watch as an Amazon delivery van parks up near our car. The van driver gets out of the vehicle, parcel in hand, and walks down the garden path of the house that Ralph has been watching so intently.

'Keep watching,' Ralph says.

The delivery man knocks on the door, which is opened by a tall and very attractive woman, who seems surprised to see the parcel, but then signs to acknowledge its receipt, before smiling and closing the door.

The delivery man gets back into his van and drives off.

I'm feeling utterly baffled, so I ask, 'Yeah, so? What the hell was I supposed to be watching out for?'

Ralph sighs wistfully, turns to me slowly, smiles cryptically and declares in measured tones, 'She's the beautiful woman I turned down, and instead I ended up marrying you.'

At first upon hearing those words, I feel like I've just become bizarrely detached from reality, because no level of reality ought to exist where such barbed words can admissibly be spoken by a husband to his wife.

We sit in hushed silence for a moment or two, while I absorb the dirty bomb of his words. Then something occurs to me, and I can't help eyeing him with an open-mouthed look of incredulous disgust.

'Was it *you* who ordered that delivery, just so you could ogle her when she opened the door? Tell me you didn't do that, because that's completely nuts!'

Ralph shakes his head and casts me a withering look. 'Of course I didn't,' he snaps. 'I mean, ok yes I did order the delivery, but obviously not to ogle her. I did it so you could see the stunner I could have had, and instead ended up being lumbered with you.'

'Who in the name of Beelzebub even does that though?' I ask him in a voice of tightly constrained croakiness, my mouth still agape. Then my eyes fill with tears, and the droplets fall down my jumper and into my lap. 'You really know how to make me feel like rubbish don't you?' I say to him, sobbing.

'Oh come on Adele, I'm merely trying to make you see the sacrifice I've made for your sake, in the hope that you'll appreciate me more, that's all.'

'How is you coming here and showing me how much you're lusting after another woman supposed to make me want to appreciate you? And how am I even supposed to believe that you know her at all? Any nutcase can order a delivery to anywhere they like. It doesn't mean you know the people who live there, does it?'

Intuitively, I know that I am splurging my words out now, and I have gone too far.

Ralph grasps the wheel and begins to drive off. There's a look of suppressed rage on his face now, which remains for the entire journey home.

I quell my tears and remain involuntarily quiet, because I would prefer to scream my dread of what I know is to come when we arrive home. The uneasy silence is punctuated only by my sniffles. Once again, I experience a strange feeling of having become detached from reality and even myself, as if being mistreated in this way could only happen in some other bizarre existence ungoverned by any sense of reality or decorum at all.

When the car pulls into our drive, I exit shakily and make my way to the front door. Once I'm over the threshold, I make my way up the stairs to the bathroom, because it's the room with the thinnest walls. Thin walls never stop him though, I think to myself in dismay.

Moments later, my face is flecked with his spittle as he roars his rage into my being. This time I suffer the onslaught not just of his fists, but his feet too. It's mainly my torso that takes the battering, where he knows the bruises will remain hidden from view.

....

I've been lying in bed now for around sixteen hours. I know because I'm able to peep at the clock on the sideboard through my gummed eyes. After yesterday's beating, I crawled into bed and I've been lying here, as still as possible. Ralph knows how unusual it is for me to lie in bed for this long. Normally I'm up after eight hours.

As for him, he's been up for hours.

Now I sense him padding furtively over to the bed. Then I feel him place two fingers on my wrist. He's checking my pulse. He keeps them there for a second or two, before padding slowly away.

A shiver runs down the length of my spine. A torrent of thoughts tumble into my mind. He's checking to see if I'm alive or dead, that's for sure. Of course, granted, a sleeping posture often has the semblance of death. But if he were genuinely concerned for my wellbeing, wouldn't he shake me gently by the shoulder to wake me and speak with me? Checking for my pulse like that is slightly unnerving, as if he's expecting me to be dead, or even - that's it - like he's *waiting for me to die, because maybe he wants me to die*. These beatings, which started not very long after we became married six months ago, have increased in frequency and intensity with each passing month. He always expresses remorse, but there's no way its authentic, because the beatings have hardly relented. And besides, the amount of time between each expression of remorse and the next beating is growing shorter and shorter.

And checking my pulse like that feels like a metaphor for the state of our marriage, too. If our marriage were to have a pulse of its own, I'm pretty sure it would be the faintest of fading palpitations.

.....

Later in the day, the time comes for me to prepare Ralph's dinner. I experience several fleeting moments during which I feel oddly disconnected from myself and my surroundings, almost as if the thought of deviating from routine expectations wouldn't matter one bit. It is on the crest of this feeling that I find myself listlessly peeling a potato. It happens to be an absolutely huge and knobbly potato. Normally I would chop it into smaller pieces before putting it into the pot on the stove to boil. But then I make a decision, as if acting not of my own volition, to pop the potato, in its whole, unchopped, monstrous rotundity, into the boiling pot.

Two minutes later, Ralph comes into the kitchen. He sees the potato.

'Why on earth haven't you sliced the potato?' he asks in exasperation.

I feel myself shrugging my shoulders, and I can feel my legs starting to feel weak at the knee.

'What do you mean you don't know? And exactly how long do you think it's going to take to cook a potato that size, you dullard?'

Once more he's raging into my face and flecking me with his spittle.

Angelina

A new patient by the name of Adele Weatherford has been admitted into Groatcrest today. Groatcrest is a mental health hospital, where I've been working for the last four years. I've been assigned as one of Adele's mental health nurses.

During my time, I've seen many patients come into Groatcrest, but I don't recall ever seeing a person in such a severe state of depression as Adele appears to be. She seems to be so depressed that it's as if her brain is almost shutting itself off. Even though she has voluntarily chosen to be admitted onto the ward, she appears to be in such a grave state that if she'd have refused to come in of her own will, she'd most likely have been admitted under what we in the mental health field call 'a section', which means being involuntarily detained against one's will. This happens when experienced psychiatrists conduct an assessment of a person's state of mind, and decide that she poses a risk to her own wellbeing and therefore needs to be hospitalised for her own safety.

Her parents were instrumental in bringing her in. They're acquainted with some medics, who were able to put them in touch with us.

Adele's been put on medication. The head psychiatrist here, Dr Harpoon, has ordered that she be put on an antidepressant called Wellbutrin. She's taking it without any fuss - sometimes people refuse it, but she didn't put up any resistance at all. To be honest, she's in such a wretched state of despondency that she probably wouldn't be able to bring herself to put up any resistance, even if she wanted to, the poor mite.

She told me she just wants to curl up in bed. That's common enough. Sometimes they just want to retreat from the world.

Adele

I'm in a psychiatric unit, charmingly named Groatcrest. I've got a basic little bedroom to myself, and a nurse by the name of Angelina has given me some pills that'll supposedly help give me a lift.

Yesterday, back at the house, I was feeling so incredibly low that I was scared I might do something stupid, because I got my hands on a load of paracetamol and other stuff. I phoned my mum and dad and asked them to come over. I didn't know what else to do. When they arrived, they saw the load of loose pills on my side table that I'd popped out of their blister packs. Mum in particular became extremely concerned, and the next thing I know, she made a few telephone calls, and then some professional looking medical people arrived at the house. They asked me some questions about my state of mind, which I answered honestly. They were concerned that I posed a danger to myself, and asked me whether I would be willing to come for a stay in hospital on a voluntary basis, so that I could be assessed more thoroughly. As I've been aching for help to take me out of the way I've been feeling, I agreed with barely a moment's hesitation.

I packed a few things and before too long, I was whisked away to this Groatcrest place in some vehicle of which, I'm annoyed to find, I have only a very poor recollection.

I hear a light knock on the door to my room. A few seconds later, Angelina enters and sees me sitting on a simple wooden chair.

'Good morning Adele,' she says cheerily. 'Great to see you showered and dressed already, that's an encouraging start to the day. I've come to take you to your appointment to see Dr Harpoon, the head psychiatrist. I know it's a bit early, but he says he's actually ready to see you now.'

'Oh, ok then,' I say weakly.

I follow her out of my room and into the hospital ward corridor. She leads me down an adjoining corridor, past many doors which I imagine lead to bedrooms like my own. Then eventually we come to an area of the ward where an office is based. We come to a standstill outside a door that bears a metal plaque, which has the name "Dr Harpoon" engraved upon it.

Angelina raps on the door sharply.

'Come in,' calls a voice from within.

Angelina opens the door widely, to reveal a neat and modern-looking office. There's a large table, behind which is sat a middle-aged man of small stature, who is dressed smartly in a tweed suit and shiny black shoes.

A faint smile hovers around his mouth and his eyes as he gazes directly at me and beckons me inside with an economical gesture of his hand.

I step tentatively inside.

'Thank you, Angelina,' says Dr Harpoon. She walks briskly away, leaving me standing there slightly awkwardly.

'It's Adele isn't it?' he asks pleasantly, but it's more of a statement than a question. 'Nice to meet you, my name's Dr Harpoon, as I'm sure you're aware. Please feel free to take a seat and make yourself comfortable. Pour yourself some cordial if you wish.' He indicates a glass jug of orange squash on the table. I find his urbane manner of talking pleasing.

I take a seat in front of his desk.

'Now, I'm very well informed concerning the circumstances of your hospital admission, Adele. How would you say you're feeling right now?'

I pause to think about how best to answer his question. 'I feel terrible, to be honest. I feel like there's pain leaking out of me. I feel really, really low.'

'I see,' he says, nodding gravely. He picks up a parker pen and starts to write on a sheet of paper in front of him, but I can't make out what he's writing because his handwriting is very small, and of course it's upside down from the perspective of where I'm sitting.

'So, would you describe your mood as being persistently very low?'

'Yes.'

'Would you say you've experienced this for two weeks or longer?'

'Oh yes, definitely, and certainly for more than two weeks.'

'Mmhm. And would you say you've lost interest in any activities that once brought you enjoyment or pleasure?'

'Yes, I'd say that's true, yes. I used to love being in nature and playing netball for a local team, but that doesn't seem to interest me any longer.'

'And this loss of interest has persisted for longer than two weeks?'

'Oh yes, for sure.'

'And would you say you've been experiencing disrupted sleep for a period of two weeks or longer? Or even a desire to sleep more than usual, or difficulty actually getting up out of bed?'

I look down at the floor a little shamefacedly. 'Well, I must admit that I have…have been staying in bed a lot longer than usual of late. I've been really struggling with facing the reality of each day.'

'For two weeks or longer?'

'Yeah.'

'Would you say you've been experiencing feelings of worthlessness?'

'Yes,' I say in a tremulous voice, after a moment's hesitation. But the reason for my hesitation has nothing to do with needing to ponder the answer to the question. It is more to do with being unprepared for the tears that welled up in my eyes when he uttered the word, "worthlessness".

'For two weeks or longer?'

'Yes,' I say, wiping away the moisture in my eyes to avert the formation of teardrops.

'And would you say that you're feeling generally lacking in energy?'

'Oh God, yes, I feel pretty listless really.'

I watch Dr Harpoon writing his notes for a few moments. The office is so quiet that I can easily hear the scratch of his pen on the surface of the paper.

'Would you say this has been the case for two weeks or longer?'

'Oh yes.'

He glances up at me and purses his lips, before casting his eyes back down towards the paper.

'And what about the circumstances that led to your parents becoming deeply concerned about you, of which I am now well-informed? Would you say that you were thinking about actively using a large quantity of paracetamol pills, mixed up with other pills, as a means of ending your life?'

'Well,' I say, casting my own eyes down towards the floor, 'I....I don't think I would have actually carried anything through, at the end of the day. I mean, I know that if I do get any stupid ideas into my head, I just need to get in touch with mum or dad or anybody really, cos as long as there's someone there with me, I won't be able to do anything silly.'

'I see. But what I'm trying to get at is: would you say that the idea of committing suicide has entered your thoughts for a period of two weeks or longer?'

I let out a long sigh. 'Yes,' I say emphatically, with a greater sense of irritation than I intended.

He puts down his pen, takes a deep breath, settles back in his chair and brings his interlocked fingers to rest on the desk in front of him.

'Ok Adele, well the symptoms you're exhibiting are clearly an indication that you're suffering from major depressive disorder, commonly referred to as clinical depression. You've already been placed on a course of an antidepressant called Wellbutrin, and during your stay here, we'll need to closely monitor how well you respond to it.'

'You're giving me a diagnosis?'

'Yes, it's a clear-cut case of major depressive disorder. The course of Wellbutrin tablets may take a few weeks to start working, but they should help to control your symptoms. You may experience some side effects such as dizziness or nausea, but that's completely normal.'

'But....when you say disorder, where did that come from?' I blurt out clumsily.

'Well Adele, major depressive disorder is a mental disorder which is biological in origin. You can think of it as a brain disease or malfunction that has a genetic component to it as well. Often there is a deficiency of important chemicals within the brain, such as a serotonin deficiency. Or you can think of it as a chemical imbalance within the brain, and I very much hope that the course of medication I'm prescribing for you will go some way towards reducing this imbalance.'

.....

Back in my room, lying on my bed, I have to say I'm feeling utterly bewildered by everything that passed between Dr Harpoon and myself during our meeting. Truthfully, I feel nothing short of infuriated by the fact that he didn't once ask me about my life, and what experiences I've been struggling with. When I told him I've been really struggling to get out of bed to face the reality of each day, it didn't seem to occur to him at all to ask me why I've been feeling this way. And when I divulged that I've been experiencing feelings of worthlessness, that's surely an admission that needs unpacking! But again, he didn't ask me at all for my opinion as to why I've been feeling this way, which seems to demonstrate that he doesn't think my opinion is important at all, and that he doesn't attach any value to any insights of my own into the reasons why I'm feeling the way I am. And of all people, I should surely be the one to have some idea as to why I'm feeling so damn terrible, shouldn't I? I mean, shouldn't Dr Harpoon be asking me about my life? If he could be bothered to ask, I would tell him what I've been wanting to reveal so desperately: the abusive treatment I've suffered at the hands of my husband. As it is, he hasn't bothered to ask about my life experiences, which surely demonstrates that he doesn't have a handle on the crucial issue here.

And there's another thing I'm feeling really irritated about. He kept asking me, over and over again, whether I've been experiencing certain feelings for two weeks or longer. I'd like to know, who the hell was it that decided that two weeks is the significant length of time to be suffering certain symptoms, as a way of determining whether someone is suffering from a mental disorder? I mean, why not ten days, or eleven days, or three weeks, or any other number for that matter? It just really smacks of arbitrariness to me! Wouldn't it be better to ask how long I've been experiencing these feelings, and what happened to me around the time that they started?

And to be honest, I think I'd have appreciated a little more compassion.

.....

One week later, I'm standing in Dr Harpoon's office again, because I've requested a second meeting.

'Good morning Adele, please close the door and take a seat,' he says. As before, I discern a faint smile that hovers around his mouth and his eyes. 'What is it I can help you with?'

I sit down in front of his desk and find myself instinctively making a movement to fold my arms, but I rein in the urge and place my hands flat in my lap.

'Well, I just have a few questions about my diagnosis, Dr Harpoon.'

He relaxes a little in his chair and tilts his head to one side, nodding. 'Yes, of course,' he says, pouring out two glasses of orange juice from the jug on the table. 'I'm very earnest to make sure all my patients here at Groatcrest are well informed and have a good grasp of their treatment plan.'

'Yes well, I'm really, really curious to know, doctor, why you haven't - well, why you didn't need to ask me anything about my life and my experiences, and how that might have a bearing on how depressed I've been feeling.'

Dr Harpoon purses his lips and leans forward animatedly. Suddenly his professional demeanour gives way to one of apologetic awkwardness.

'I'm sorry, ever so sorry Adele if I seemed a little impersonal or incurious upon our first meeting. Sometimes that can be an upshot of my method, which is strongly focused on examining clusters of symptoms as a means of establishing a diagnosis. But really, please feel free, be my guest, is there something on your mind that you'd like to discuss with me?'

'Well, last time when I told you I've been feeling really terribly low and worthless, well...I think - I think it's got everything to do with my relationship with my husband Ralph.'

Dr Harpoon nods encouragingly, although his face is frowning. 'Ok, tell me about your relationship with you husband.'

'Well, Ralph has this habit of insisting on showing me photos in which he's posing with women from his past, with whom he claims to have been romantically involved, and then he compares me to them in an unfavourable light, making downright brazenly insulting comments about me all the time. And whenever he does so, he makes me feel utterly belittled.'

'I'm sorry to hear that, Adele.'

'It's like he's got this weird obsession of comparing me with other women all the time, as a way of hurting me. And sometimes he'll go to ridiculous lengths to do it. The other day, we went out for a spin in the car together, and he parked outside this house that I'd never seen before. He was just sitting there watching the house, until an Amazon delivery van arrived to deliver a parcel there. We both watched as a woman answered the door, signed for the parcel and went back inside. Then he turned to me with this weird smile and told me this same woman was a beautiful lady he turned down, and instead he ended up marrying me. Then I accused Ralph of ordering the parcel himself, just so that he could get a brief chance of ogling her, and do you know what he said? He admitted he ordered the parcel himself, claiming that he just wanted me to see the stunner he could have chosen to be with, in place of myself.'

At my recollection of the event, tears spring in my eyes and I find myself giving in to the impulse to weep.

Dr Harpoon rises from his seat and walks over to me.

'There, there,' he says solicitously, before offering me a handkerchief from his top pocket.

'Thank you,' I say, accepting it with a whimper.

'He told me some nonsense about wanting me to see the sacrifice he'd made for my sake, so that I would appreciate him more,' I continue, once he has returned to his seat behind his desk. 'And then I told him any nutcase can order a delivery to any random place, but it doesn't mean he knows the people who live there, so I was basically implying that he had staged the whole thing by pretending to know her. That made him really angry. When we got home, he battered me really badly, doctor. Punching and kicking me. It was horrendous.'

I stand up, turn around and lift up my top, exposing the bruises on my sides and back, which are unmistakably expansive, albeit no longer fresh.

'It's a pattern of mental and physical abuse, because it's happened countless times now,' I tell him. 'But it's been getting gradually worse the whole time, increasing in frequency and severity. For a while now, I've been feeling unloved, confused, fearful, utterly dejected and ashamed.

I'm spiralling down into hopelessness and helplessness, because I feel trapped - I'll tell you for why. A few months ago, I tried to leave him, but he tracked me down. He has a forcefully persuasive way of making me stay. I can't see an easy way out of this at all.'

'I'm sorry to hear you've had such a trying time, Adele. It must have been really hard for you.'

'Well, that's the crux of what I'm trying to say, you see, doctor. You're telling me I'm suffering from major depressive disorder because of some brain disease or genetic malfunction, or some sort of chemical imbalance, but to my mind, my feelings of distress are an understandable reaction to the abuse I'm suffering at the hands of my husband, not a consequence of some brain disease or genetic flaw. Surely what I need is some sort of professional team who can offer practical assistance in supporting my decision to get a divorce from Ralph, so I can move away and sever contact from him. I'm convinced that would help me to feel ten thousand times better.'

Dr Harpoon clears his throat noisily.

'Adele, I really do feel a lot of sympathy for you, in terms of what you say you've been through with your husband. But there's something very important I need you to try to understand. I've established that you're suffering from major depressive disorder, and I need you to grasp that it is a brain disease which has a biological origin or cause. Factors such as an adverse home life or having a husband who is prone to behaving unpleasantly can be stressors in themselves, but the great majority of us are able to cope with these ordinary stresses that life throws at us.' Dr Harpoon's voice has become firm and emphatic. 'Now here's the thing, Adele. People who are suffering from a major depressive disorder have an underlying biological vulnerability to the stresses of everyday life, to the extent that these ordinary stresses can become overwhelming. So, when considering the question of the causation of your suffering, it is the underlying brain disease to which we must attribute primacy.'

I spend a moment thinking about his words, but I'm feeling very baffled.

'So, forgive me, let me get this right doctor,' I say, not quite managing to resist imparting an acerbic edge to my voice, 'you're basically saying there's a strong possibility that the reason I'm feeling so distressed, dejected and fearful, and all the other cocktail of emotions, isn't down to the abusive treatment perpetrated against me by my husband, because most people would just expect to deal with that as part of everyday life.

It's down to an underlying biological vulnerability instead. Is that basically what you're saying?'

'I think you've deliberately chosen to subtly alter my words, Adele, if you don't mind me saying so. I'm not trying to say its normal for a woman to expect to be mistreated by her husband. Not at all. I'm saying most people have the mental strength to cope with these adverse experiences, but those individuals who have an underlying biological vulnerability such as major depressive disorder become easily overwhelmed and horribly dispirited.'

'Mmm,' I say sceptically. 'So I see now why, during our first meeting, you didn't bother to ask me about my experiences. Apparently, it's pretty much immaterial that I've suffered mental and physical abuse at the hands of my husband.' I eye Dr Harpoon pointedly and adopt a tone of overblown cheeriness. 'I say, that's really very, very handy for Ralph isn't it?'

Dr Harpoon shuffles a little in his seat and lets out an impatient sigh.

'I know it's a lot to take in in one sitting, Adele. Why don't you try sleeping on it, and maybe it'll make more sense to you in the morning? Now if you don't mind, I have other patients to see, and our time has already overrun.'

I have no choice but to leave his office in a state of impotent exasperation.

Angelina

Adele's been here at Groatcrest for nearly a month now.

It is proving very difficult to get her to show any desire to participate in any of the social activities that we run within the hospital ward. I ask her whether she would like to do flower arranging, cooking, board games, or yoga, but she isn't interested in doing anything on offer here.

She spends a great deal of her time in a deeply depressed state of mind. The poor mite's in such a wretched state of melancholy that when she's sitting in the ward's communal area with the other patients, she just sits silently and doesn't interact with anyone, apart from when she displays intermittent bursts of anger, during which she outspokenly denounces Dr Harpoon and the diagnosis of major depressive disorder he's given her. In fact, she'll denounce him to anyone who'll listen, which includes both patients and other nurses.

Today it's a Tuesday afternoon, and she's made a real effort, because she's wearing her best dress and styled her hair very nicely. Right now, I'm standing in the ward's corridor, observing her sitting in the communal area, where most of the ten patients in attendance are receptively listening to one of her tirades.

'Doctor Harpoon is a fraud who says I'm suffering from a brain disease called major depressive disorder,' she is saying, gesticulating with palms turned upwards in the air. 'I told him my distressed state and feelings of hopelessness are a consequence of the mental and physical abuse my husband's been putting me through, rather than any underlying brain condition. I told Dr Harpoon I need a team of people to offer me practical assistance in getting away from my husband and getting a divorce, which will surely spur my recovery, because it's my toxic relationship with my husband that's been the source of all my hurt and distress. But Dr Harpoon insists I have an underlying brain disease that makes me vulnerable to those everyday stresses of life that most other people would be able to cope with. He says this underlying brain disease or major depressive disorder means I'll find these everyday stresses overwhelming. Do you know the thing that makes me feel really angry, guys? Huh? He actually has the nerve to characterise the mental and physical abuse I've suffered at the hands of my husband as ordinary stresses that the great majority of us are able to cope with, but because I supposedly have this depressive disorder, I am prone to being overwhelmed and emotionally broken by such stresses. Well, I'm sorry, but I don't think that's truthful at all, guys. I think it's totally misguided and, well - crazy - to characterise a pattern of systematic mental and physical abuse as the ordinary stresses of life. It's just such a point of view that can conceal and perpetuate such abuse, if you ask me. What I've been through are, in fact, extraordinary circumstances, and my distress is a perfectly understandable reaction to it. I mean, I've tried leaving him, for Pete's sake, but he has a knack of tracking me down and making me stay. I'm firmly of the opinion that the great majority of people would become extremely distressed, just like me, if they experienced what I've been through, and becoming overwhelmed by it is not an indicator of some underlying special vulnerability stemming from some brain disease. And I'd bet my last penny that the distress that all of you guys are going through is an understandable reaction to the individual circumstances of your own lives, rather than some brain disease, like these psychiatrists are trying to tell us. They're trying to hoodwink us.'

I don't like to admit it, and Dr Harpoon isn't here to respond to these accusations, but Adele makes a good argument. You can't deny that.

One of the patients, a woman named Francesca, stands up excitedly. 'You know what's always bugged me?' she says with a flourish of her hand. 'Dr Harpoon's never bothered to ask me about what's happened in my life, and whether that played a part in my depression. He's just never asked! It's always puzzled me.'

'Yes, Francesa, you're quite right to bring that up,' Adele says, mirroring her enthusiasm. 'Dr Harpoon hasn't half got a neck on him! Since he characterises the systematic mental and physical abuse I've been going through as everyday stresses that most people would be able to cope with, yet as something that overwhelms me because of some made-up brain disease that makes me especially vulnerable, it's a way of thinking that conveniently excuses him from examining too closely either the experiences and events that led to my distressed state or their meaning to me. This diagnosis of major depressive disorder he's slammed me with is a sham, because it decontextualises and pathologises my distress by practically ignoring all the abuse I've been through! And trying to make out that my distress is down to something going haywire in my genes or my brain diminishes and obscures the reality of the devastating experiences that've led to my distress, and that's tantamount to collusion and complicity with the perpetrator of the abuse, my damn, bloody husband!'

'I think you've got a damn good point there, Adele,' says Francesca. 'It's music to my ears, absolute gold dust, because I've kind of been thinking it myself, but didn't quite know how to say it.'

'Do you know what though Francesca, Dr Harpoon actually had the nerve to say that most people have got the mental strength to cope with abuse from their husbands, unlike me,' Adele scoffs. 'It's like he's saying I'm mentally weak because of this fictional brain disease I'm supposed to have. That's absolute tosh. I tell you, the kind of systematic abuse I've been dealing with is exactly the kind that'll take the great majority of people's strength away, and it certainly can't be assumed that I'm weak for being so enfeebled by it.'

.....

Later that same day, I knock on the door to Adele's room.

'Come in,' I hear her call in a groggy voice.

I go in and see her lying in bed, bleary-eyed.

'Sorry to disturb you Adele,' I say gently. I move over to her bedside and sit alongside her on a stool.

'How are you feeling?' I ask.

'Pretty terrible really,' she replies with a little whimper and an attempt at a wry smile.

'I was wondering, since you seem to be very open to talking about your experiences,' I venture tentatively, 'whether you would like to talk about the abuse that you've been through, since they say a problem shared can be a problem halved?'

I feared that she might find the question intrusive, but I'm relieved to discover that she's very willing to talk about what she's been through. She tells me all about how her husband has been denigrating her by regularly comparing her unfavourably to other women, and that he will even go to very strange lengths to do so, as if he has an obsessive preoccupation with it. She gives me a detailed account of regular beatings that she's suffered, which is painful for me to listen to.

'And on one occasion, my husband arrived home from work while I was in the middle of having a panic attack,' Adele says, tears welling in her eyes. 'My heart was pounding, I had this horrible shortness of breath, I was visibly trembling, and I was feeling an intense sense of fear and discomfort. Anyone could see straight away that I was suffering. I told him I was having a panic attack, and do you know what he did, Angelina? He just said, "Oh, I'm going out". A second after arriving home, he was back out the door. Probably went down the pub.'

I feel appalled by what I'm hearing. I've heard many unsavoury accounts of mistreatment and neglect since I began my career as a mental health nurse, but this account of her husband deserting her while she was in the throes of a panic attack seems particularly callous to me.

'Oh, my poor dear,' I say, patting her shoulder gently, 'that does sound quite uncaring to me. I mean, I have experience of being around people having panic attacks, and when they start to tremble and turn pale, it tends to elicit in me a very strong impulse to be with them and try to soothe them. Being around someone who's having a panic attack is a very visceral experience, and I imagine most people's response would be a caring one, you know, to stick around and try to help out in whatever way they can. To simply leave them to it does seem remarkably uncaring, I must say.'

'Thank you, thank you,' Adele says emphatically. I can see that she appreciates my understanding and sympathy.

'The only thing I can possibly think someone might try to say to justify deserting the scene,' I say, pondering aloud, 'would be, "oh, I can't stand seeing someone suffering like that," but from what you've told me about your husband, that's probably an unlikely explanation.'

'You're right there, not bloody likely,' she laughs bitterly.

'Well my dear, how about we book you in for an appointment with Mr Kaneary, the ward's trauma therapist, to see if he can provide you with some level of support. He's only recently been appointed, but I've heard nothing but positive stuff about him. What do you say?'

'Well it might be worth a shot, I suppose,' Adele says, shrugging her shoulders.

Adele

Angelina secured an appointment for me with Mr Kaneary for the very next day.

I enter his office and take a seat opposite him. He's a bespectacled man dressed in casual smart clothes. He's smiling warmly.

'So, tell me a little bit about what's happened in your life that's led to you landing up here?' he asks.

It's a refreshing question for sure, not least because he sounds genuinely interested in what I have to say.

I tell him in great detail about the pattern of mentally and physically abusive behaviour Ralph has perpetrated against me. I find him to be a receptive listener.

'Is this the first time in your life that you've suffered abuse of this nature?'

'No, it isn't,' I say after a small pause.

'That doesn't surprise me at all, because often we can find that certain life experiences recur throughout our lives, although most of the time we're oblivious to the possibility that it can be our own mindset that leads us to a pattern of repeated experiences. Would you like to tell me about the first time this happened to you?'

'Yes, ok.' He's engaging, and I want to tell him, because I've never told anyone about my early experiences of abuse before, and I feel very strongly that its high time that I did. There is a tenacious part of me that wants to resist divulging my secret, but after a momentary tussle, that part is overcome.

'Well, when I was a child, my mother was often ill, and my father was often abroad in a different country on business trips. So there were periods of my childhood when this adult relative in my life felt obliged to look after me. Often, I got the impression that he felt he'd been lumbered with me. I experienced some pretty extreme acts of violence from this adult. On one occasion, he strangled me with an electrical cord.'

Tears well up in my eyes. I make no attempt to hold them back.

'It grieves me to hear that Adele, no child should have to suffer that level of mistreatment. Is this the first time you've spoken about it?'

'Yes.'

'And tell me, saying this extreme act of violence out loud and attaching it to an adult in your life - an adult who should have been caring for you, how does that feel?'

'If I'm honest with you, saying it out loud feels weirdly like I'm betraying the guy who carried out these violent acts. I mean, of course it's wrong for an adult to be strangling a child, one hundred per cent. It would be crazy to try to blame the child. I know that adult in my life was in the wrong. But still, I'm getting this weird feeling that somehow I'm betraying him by speaking it out loud, and in actual fact, it was me….it was me who was to blame for what happened.'

'From one angle it does seem weird that you feel you're betraying him,' Mr Kaneary says softly, 'since it's completely the other way around - in reality, he betrayed you, very badly. But from another angle, these feelings are completely understandable. When you're a child, you have very little power to change any violent or abusive situation you're involved with at the hands of an adult. It's not like you can move away, or make the person stop hurting you. So you've got two options. You can admit to yourself how powerless you are, and that you can do nothing about the fact that you're being hurt. That option can make you feel unbearably powerless. The other option is to tell yourself it's your own fault. If you do that, you at least gain some sense of power, if only in your own mind. If it's your fault, you feel there's actually something you can do to make it better or different. When you're a child, you take the second option to avoid that frightening position of powerlessness offered by the first option. If you blame yourself for your childhood traumas, it protects you from seeing how vulnerable you were and are. There's a sense that if you believe it's your fault, it feels under your control.'

'Wow, that does strike a chord with me, actually,' I say, finding myself stirred by his words.

'Now but here's the thing, Adele. That second option comes at a huge price. If you believe you were responsible for being hurt because it was your fault, then at some level, it's likely that there's a core part of you that feels defective and therefore believes you deserved it. A person who believes they're defective at their core and that they deserved to be hurt as a child isn't going to think they deserve much as an adult, either. As a child, telling yourself you were to blame for what was happening was actually a vital survival mechanism. But if you carry that mindset into your adult life, it's something that has long outlived its usefulness, and its misfiring now. In fact, there can be a lot of misplaced shame attached to believing that there's something defective at the core of your person. And shame is a very poisonous emotion. There is strong research evidence that traumatic childhoods often produce adults who are prone to suffering depression. I strongly believe that is linked to holding onto those misplaced feelings of shame, but recovery can come from fully realising that the blame can only be attributed to the perpetrator of the abuse, which leads to feelings of shame being released.'

'Honestly, I can't even begin to tell you how much sense this is making to me!'

I feel like throwing my arms around Mr Kaneary. I almost do, but I'm restrained by the thought of how inappropriate it would be.

'And do you know what, Adele? This is really crucial now, you understand. Remember when I said earlier that certain life experiences can recur throughout our lives, because own mindset leads us to a pattern of repeated experiences? Well, now you'll hopefully have a handle on what I mean. If you continue to misattribute blame to yourself for what happened to you as a child, and continue to mistakenly believe that there's something defective or shameful at your core, and mistakenly believe that you deserved it, and mistakenly believe that you don't deserve very much from life, then you'll tend to find yourself settling for relationships with people who are uncaring and don't fulfil your need to be loved, who may even behave in abusive ways towards you, just like your husband. It can all become a pattern of recurring experiences because you think you don't deserve much better. And that's what's perpetuating your feelings of depression. But you can break this cycle of abusive relationships by releasing any sense of shame that you may be holding onto at your core, which will lead on to the possibility of recovery and a much more fulfilling life.'

Tears are streaming down my face now.

'It wasn't your fault, Adele,' says Mr Kaneary gently. 'Remember it wasn't your fault. There's no need to feel ashamed any more.'

Angelina

Since Adele had her appointment with Mr Kaneary a week ago, she continues to spend an awful lot of her time in bed, in a deeply depressed state of mind. But her outspoken denunciation of Dr Harpoon in front of the other patients is becoming more frequent now, and that's in part down to new insights she's gained from Mr Kaneary.

It's a Wednesday afternoon today, and Adele's put on a lovely dress and spent a while styling her hair, no doubt to make herself stand out as much as possible. I'm standing in the ward's corridor, just like before, observing her sitting in the ward's communal area, where there's a gathering of patients, some of whom appear to be captivated by what she's saying.

'Mr Kaneary is an absolute Godsend, really he is,' she says, fizzing with admiration. 'He's given me a brilliant insight into how early childhood experiences of abuse at the hands of a relative who was supposed to be looking after me, has had negative long-term effects on my life. He's helped me to understand that all this time, I've been holding on to a false narrative that the abuse was my fault, and that it happened because there's something fundamentally wrong with me in a bad way, and so I must have deserved it. He helped me to see that I've been holding onto this sense of shame inside, thinking I'm a worthless person. So, the distress and depression I've been feeling is a consequence of both traumatic childhood experiences and also this lingering sense of shame that I kept hidden all this time. But he's helped me to see that I can learn to attribute that shame to the perpetrator, where it belongs. I can't emphasise enough, guys, how good it felt to open up about something for the first time in my life - something of which I'd been feeling ashamed - and find that I'm accepted regardless. And there's something else guys. He's helped me to understand that holding onto mistaken feelings of shame has led me to get into relationships with low down scumbags, because I don't feel like I deserve any better! Scumbags who carry out traumatic abuse, just like my husband, thereby contributing to the perpetuation of a cycle of abuse and depression! How ironic can you get!'

'My God, he's a very clever man, that Mr Kaneary,' says one patient by the name of Fiona. 'Every time I have a session with him, he keeps telling me that my own depression is a response to what I've been through in my life, and I can heal from it in time.'

'Yes Fiona,' Adele replies enthusiastically, 'Mr Kaneary should be running this place, because he's a million times better than Dr Harpoon

Mr Kaneary understands, on a fundamental level, that the key question is "What's happened to you?" and not "What's wrong with you?" I've told Dr Harpoon that my distress is a consequence of abusive experiences, but he obstinately persists in believing that I'm suffering from an underlying brain disease or major depressive disorder. That diagnosis of major depressive disorder he slammed me with is a ridiculous sham, because it excuses him from examining the experiences that led to my distressed state in the first place. If it was up to him, I would never have discovered the all-important finding that all this time I've been mistakenly taking on board this poisonous sense of shame, which ought to be firmly laid at the door of my childhood abuser. I would never have discovered my need to release all this shame as a means of healing from my distress. I mean, Dr Harpoon may as well be shaking hands with my abusers! That's how damned useless I find his diagnosis!'

The gathering of patients reacts with a blend of nervous laughter, nods of approval, and murmurs of agreement. One patient gives a louder cry of 'Here, here!'

.....

Early In the evening, when Adele has returned to her room, I go to check on her to see how she's doing.

I'm sitting by her bedside.

'Oh, I'm feeling quite tired and exhausted - it must be all that talking I've been doing,' she says with a little yawn. Then she gives a shake of her head, rousing herself and propping herself up in her bed. 'You know you asked me whether I'd like to talk about what I've been through with my husband the other day, Angelina? A problem shared is a problem halved, as you say?'

'Yes? What would you like to tell me, Adele?'

'Well, wait till you hear this one. Several months ago, I organised a surprise party for my husband's birthday. It took a hell of a lot of organising, particularly all the food preparation. When he arrived home from work that day, there were around fifty friends and acquaintances waiting to wish him a happy birthday. "Surprise!" they all cried in unison. Admittedly, he looked a little bit taken aback at first, but that's kind of like the point, right? He soon appeared to get into the party swing. But he barely talked to me all night, and he didn't talk to me at all for a month afterwards. A month! Not one single word. I mean, clearly he doesn't like surprises or parties, but how was I supposed to know that? If he'd have warned me about the fact that he doesn't like parties, and then I went ahead and organised one anyway, I'd be able to understand his resentment, because I'd be going against his express wishes. But he hadn't given any intimation to that effect at all.'

'Oh Adele, I think his cold silent treatment was excessively harsh by any standard,' I say sympathetically.

'Thank you, Angelina, you're a good listener.'

'But, would I be right in saying that behaviour pales in comparison to the physical abuse he meted out to you?'

Adele looks thoughtful for a moment, and then intensely sad. 'Yes, true,' she replies, 'but then again, there is something uniquely callous about actively deciding not to acknowledge your wife for a period of a month, for doing something that was actually really well-intentioned.'

I find Adele's account of mistreatment and abuse at the hands of her husband deeply uncomfortable to listen to sometimes, but I also feel it's important that she talks about it.

Adele

I've requested a meeting with Dr Harpoon, because I think it's about time I left this tiresome place. Its ten o' clock on a Thursday morning. I rap on the door of his office.

'Come in,' I hear his voice promptly reply.

This time when I open the door and move over the threshold, I make sure there's no tentativeness in my step. I'm feeling very earnest about getting my point across to him.

Dr Harpoon is sitting behind his large table, once again smartly attired in a tweed suit and shiny black shoes.

'Hello again Adele,' he says urbanely, 'Please take a seat. Help yourself to orange juice, and make yourself comfortable. What is it I can do for you?' As before, his visage bears a faint smile that hovers around his mouth and eyes.

I take a seat and decide to get straight to the point.

'Yes, doctor, well I've been thinking that I'd like to bring my stay at Groatcrest to an end now, really. To be honest with you, the only intervention I've found beneficial during my stay here has been my session with Mr Kaneary. In fact, he's been absolutely illuminating and given me a great deal of invaluable insight into my own distress. I think the way forward is for me to leave here, extricate myself from my husband, and continue my sessions with Mr Kaneary as an outpatient. I see Mr Kaneary's trauma therapy as being a key contributor to my healing and recovery. But I've decided I must get back to the big wide world as soon as possible.'

Dr Harpoon frowns markedly and clears his throat. He rubs his lower lip gently with a forefinger and gazes directly at me.

'And what makes you think you're well enough to leave the hospital, Adele, If you don't mind me asking?'

There's a sudden firmness in his demeanour that's somewhat surprising.

'Well, I do still feel very down and distressed, I'll be honest, but I don't see how being in here is going to help me in any way....'

'Let me tell you something, Adele,' Dr Harpoon interrupts, leaning towards me across the table as far as he can, 'you'll remember that during our recent first meeting together, you said that you were in a terrible state and pain was leaking out of you. I've got the details written down right here. The day before your admission to Groatcrest, your parents were deeply concerned that you were considering making an attempt on your own life by taking a large amount of paracetamol pills.'

'But I told you, doctor, I don't think I'd have actually taken the pills. It was more of a cry for help really and…..'

'I feel it would be most unwise to minimise what happened,' he says, interrupting me again. 'After all, you went as far as taking the pills out of their blister packs, according to your parents' testimony. And most tellingly of all, when I asked you whether the idea of committing suicide has entered your thoughts for a period of two weeks or longer, you replied in the affirmative, did you not?'

'Well yes, but I'm not really having thoughts of this nature any more,' I say impatiently.

'But, as I'm sure you can appreciate Adele, it would be irresponsible and unwise of me to support your discharge from hospital, so soon after you made such a grave and telling admission. If you'll permit me to speak frankly, Adele, I'm unable to support your discharge from hospital because there's a substantial possibility that you may still pose a risk to yourself.'

'Doctor, please listen to me. That was more of a cry for help than a real intention to do myself harm, seriously.'

'Ahh but you were giving it enough consideration to have to phone your mum and dad and ask them to come over,' Dr Harpoon interjected briskly, 'which suggests you needed them to be there to make sure you didn't do something you shouldn't.'

The faint smile hovering around his mouth and eyes disappears for a moment, and his face takes on a resolute expression.

'No, not so much to make sure I didn't do something,' I retort in exasperation, 'but to make it known to mum and dad how desperately I needed help - like I say, it was a cry for help!'

'You see, I think you have rationalised that explanation in order to avoid becoming aware of the unpalatable truth - that you were in such a vulnerable state of mind that day, that you were capable of doing anything. I remember you saying that if you get any ideas of that nature come into your head, you need someone with you, such as your parents, to stop you from doing anything silly. Do you remember saying that?'

'Yes, but like I say, that was then, and this is now, things have changed….'

'Have they really changed though Adele?' he intercedes energetically, bringing the interlocked fingers of his clasped hands down in a controlled fashion onto the table. 'What if those kinds of ideas return, and for whatever reason, you find it difficult to contact your parents in your hour of need? What then? At least if you're in hospital, you'll always have someone close at hand to help you, won't you? In hospital, we can mitigate the risk you pose to yourself, and that is my primary responsibility right now. Your state of mind precludes any possibility of being released at the moment, I'm afraid.'

'What do you mean?' I ask incredulously.

'Angelina has reported that you've been spending a great deal of time in bed, in a deeply depressed state of mind. She tells me you've been in such a dejected state that you haven't been able to participate in any of the organised social activities on the hospital ward. And I'm told that there's often been times when you've been in the communal areas with the other patients, and you've felt so low that you haven't really been able to socialise. All this demonstrates a grave level of melancholia that needs to be treated here in the hospital. We need to try to get you functioning again, as it were.'

'And....what, so you reckon you have authority to keep me here?' I ask, still incredulous.

'I'd much, much rather that you continue to remain here on a voluntary basis, Adele, honestly I would,' says Dr Harpoon, frowning and lowering his voice a little. 'Since you're not well enough to leave, and owing to your current state of mind, if you try to discharge yourself, I'd be compelled to detain you under what's called a mental health 'section', on the grounds that you potentially pose a risk to your own wellbeing.'

'I can't believe I'm hearing this,' I say, shaking my head and scoffing. 'And how exactly do you plan to get me functioning again, as you put it? Those Wellbutrin pills you've been giving me in here haven't been doing me any good at all. And it's no wonder, because how can a pill tackle the underlying reasons that are driving my distress? And what are those reasons? Well, number one - feelings of shame and blame arising from experiences of abuse from my childhood that I've misattributed to myself rather than to the perpetrators of that abuse. And number two - low self-esteem associated with those feelings of shame and self-blame making me feel like I'm undeserving of a good life, which therefore leads me to unwisely settle for uncaring partners, like my husband, who perpetrate abusive behaviour, similar to that which I experienced during my childhood. Mr Kaneary will back me up on that score. And another thing, those Wellbutrin pills have been giving me horrible side effects. Ever since I've been on them, I've been having headaches and constipation, two things I've never been prone to - until now, that is. And you acknowledge that I've been in a deeply depressed state of mind, and you want to get me functioning again, as you put it. That implies that you're readily admitting that the pills aren't working. And it's about time you realised the reason they're not working is because they're designed to treat a brain disease that doesn't exist!'

'On the contrary, Adele, if you are finding your current medication to be of little benefit, it does not imply the absence of a brain malady,' Dr Harpoon stated unflappably, 'it merely means we need to try you on something a little more...suitable, shall we say. Since we've been monitoring you very closely while you've been taking the Wellbutrin, we've been able to establish that your particular major depressive disorder is proving very resistant to medication. So I propose that the next step is to try a course of ECT, which is short for Electroconvulsive therapy.'

I look at Dr Harpoon aghast.

'You what?' I blurt out. 'Oh no, no, no, not that thing where you get zapped with electricity? Surely, that's ever so drastic isn't it?'

'Relax, you've probably heard misleading horror stories from the early days of its use in the 1950s, when it was administered without anaesthetic,' he says in a reassuring voice. 'These days it's always given under a general anaesthetic, so there's no danger you'll be awake during treatment. Allow me to give you a very clear explanation of what Electroconvulsive therapy is, so that you're not in any doubt. I'd rather you didn't think of it as being zapped, that makes it sound like something aggressive, whereas really it can be very beneficial for people with major depressive disorder. When you're under anaesthetic, an electric current will be sent through your brain, causing a brief surge of electrical activity.'

'Yeah, like I said, you get zapped.'

'Honestly, people who've had ECT report that they find it helpful,' he says with an impatient sigh. 'I think it could be exactly the intervention that shifts the blackness of your depression. And I'll tell you what Adele: if, following the ECT, we see a demonstrable lifting of your spirits and improvement in your wellbeing, and a greater willingness to participate in the social activities on the hospital ward, I imagine I'll be much more inclined to consider you suitable for discharge from hospital. How does that sound?'

I look at him quizzically, before sarcastically saying, 'Well, it sounds like music to my ears, except - no wait - it sounds like you're saying, "no zap, no discharge". And, just enlighten me - how exactly is that different to being blackmailed?'

'Come on, Adele,' he grins defensively, 'you certainly know how to twist my words, don't you, I'll give you that, hey? I'm merely saying ECT could be the intervention that offers a real jumpstart to your recovery, that's all. Come on, what do you say?'

'I'll think about it, ok. Just let me give it some thought.'

Angelina

Still Adele languishes here at Groatcrest. It's now been five weeks since she underwent five bouts of ECT, and its plainly had some horrible effects on her.

As for myself, I've been away on a training course and I've taken some annual leave, which means this is the first time I've seen Adele since the ECT.

Adele's like a different person now.

I'm with her in her room. She's wearing her dressing gown, standing unsteadily on her feet. The waist tie of the dressing gown is working itself loose. Her hands are trembling as she slowly takes hold of the ends of the waist tie, and she makes an ineffectual looping motion with one over the other. It is as though she has completely lost the ability to tie the two ends, or entirely forgotten how to do it.

Then she drops the two ends and begins to shuffle in the direction of the en suite bathroom.

'Won goiler,' she says in a voice that sounds slurred like that of someone in an advanced state of drunkenness. However, I've smelt her breath and checked her room for alcohol, and found no evidence of boozing.

Adele reaches the bathroom but her shoulder collides with the doorframe, halting her progress.

'Won goiler,' she says again, in an irritable tone of voice.

I move closer to help her. She doesn't seem to be able to negotiate the doorframe to get into the bathroom. I take her gently by the arm and help her over the threshold, sitting her down on the toilet. She almost falls off, but I catch her.

'Adele, make sure you use the toilet grab rails to give you balance and help you get up once you've finished,' I say. I find that I'm suddenly using a tone of voice I normally reserve for elderly people or people with learning disabilities - but then there's no getting away from the fact that she is moving like an elderly person with mobility issues, and she is behaving in ways similar to a person with learning disabilities. She's a far cry from the articulate Adele I knew prior to the ECT.

I move over to the other side of the room to give her some privacy, but keep the door open so that I can hear if she's coping ok.

'Ohearybin, I've finish oww,' I hear her slur, around five minutes later.

I move closer to see. She's standing up, with both hands grasping hold of the grab rails, over which she's bending in an ungainly posture with her head bowed right down.

I take her gently by the arm and guide her back into the bedroom, so that she need not struggle with negotiating the doorframe.

I lower her down so that she can sit on the foot of the bed. But as soon as I release her and step away, her body lolls to one side and she disappears off the end of the bed, landing on the carpet.

'Oh, Adele!'

Thankfully she appears unharmed. She chortles and pushes herself up into a sitting position, so that her legs are outstretched on the floor.

'Dunno waah's makka wivvee rooay,' she says incoherently. 'Lie forgarr how to sear dow.'

I find myself looking at her ruefully and heaving a heavy sigh.

I sit down next to her on the floor, look her right in the eyes and take hold of her hand.

'Adele, do you know where you are?'

Her eyes strafe from left to right and she nods up and down several times.

'Bedroo,' she says, pointing at the bed and making distinct shapes with her mouth to form the sound of the word.

'No, but I mean, you're in a…you're in a hospital, Adele. Do you remember why you're here?'

'Hospita?' she says with a puzzled expression. She puts her hand to her head and frowns. 'I dunnoo, car memember.'

I have an idea and take out an assortment of coins from my pocket and place them on the carpet in front of her. I want to try to check her mathematical reasoning ability.

'Adele, can you do me a favour and show me what coins add up to one pound and fifty pence please?'

I recall her telling me, prior to the ECT, that she loves maths.

She brushes the coins away with a trembling palm and shakes her head sadly.

…..

Ten minutes later I'm standing outside Dr Harpoon's office. I rap on the door.

I hear footsteps from within, then the door opens wide.

'Oh hullo Angelina, how are you?' he greets me, smiling. 'How was your time off?'

'May I come in, Dr Harpoon?'

'Why, of course yes, you're in luck, you've caught me at a good time. Come in, sit yourself down.'

He closes the door and we each take seat.

'Do you mind if we skip over the small talk, Dr Harpoon?' I say hurriedly. I'm self-consciously aware that I must look visibly agitated.

'I beg your pardon?' he says with a frown, his mouth dropping open.

'It's Adele, doctor. I've just been attending to her in her room. You must know, she's in an absolutely bloody awful state. Let me ask you, how many fully-grown people do you know who've forgotten overnight how to tie their own dressing gown? Well, she has! And her hands are constantly shaking now. Her speech is slurred like a drunkard, and she's lost all her articulacy and eloquence. Her physical coordination is so bad that she can't even walk through a door without hitting the door frame. And I'll bet that her brain's so fried that she can't even remember that she's supposed to be able to walk through a doorway without colliding with the doorframe! And I just watched her sit down on her bed and fall right off it onto the carpet, her physical coordination's that off! And I've just asked her to perform a simple mathematical task using coins. She couldn't do it at all, when I know damn well that she loves maths! But here's the most outrageous thing, right. I've just asked her whether she knows where she is and why she's here. And she couldn't remember anything. She didn't even know she was in hospital until I told her.'

'Angelina, I'm strug...'

'Oh come on, doctor, don't play ignorant with me!' I say in exasperation. 'Adele is showing signs of severe brain damage. She's like a completely different person who can no longer string two sentences together. It's the ECT. She's been given far too high a dose. How many ohms of electricity has she been given, for God's sake?'

'Now I must ask you to keep a civil tongue, Angelina,' he says, firm and unruffled. 'ECT is a standard treatment for patients who've fallen into a deep depression, as well you know, and can be a very effective treatment. Now then - I'll grant you that Adele has been behaving strangely of late, with her slurred speech and physical antics, but I'll wager she's putting it on, for sure. Its manipulative and attention-seeking behaviour, characteristic of a patient who's exhibiting signs of a personality disorder. There's absolutely no evidence that her behaviour is a consequence of ECT. What I do know is that she's very keen to be discharged from hospital, but she knows we can't consider discharge until we observe a marked improvement in her symptoms, of which we've seen little evidence as yet, I'm afraid. So in the meantime, she's trying it on with these strange antics, but what she's hoping to achieve, I haven't got the foggiest idea.'

'I can't believe what I'm hearing! A person doesn't just start feigning behaviour like that! It's clearly the effects of having her brain frazzled! You can't just try to cover it up by saying she's exhibiting a personality disorder, that's ridiculous. And what about her memory loss? I suppose you think she's feigning that too! But why would she suddenly pretend to have no memory of where she is or why she's here, when she's been very enthusiastic and emphatic in speaking out about her belief that she's ended up here as a result of the abuse she's suffered at the hands of her husband? Admit it, doctor, the truth is that the ECT has erased her memory!'

'Now look here, Angelina, if you don't mind me saying so, you're being awfully presumptuous,' he says, although he still appears to be unruffled. 'I must ask you to remember your place here as a mental health nurse. I pride myself on being as tolerant and easy-going a guy as you'd wish to meet, but this is going beyond the pail now, it really is.' He leans in towards me slightly, a sickly smile hovering around his mouth, and speaks with a hint of playfulness. 'It's as if you're starting to exhibit the signs of a personality disorder yourself.'

I recoil from him, but refuse to allow myself to be intimidated.

'I know your game, doctor,' I snarl at him with a shudder, 'I'm wise to what you're doing, and I refuse to be wilfully silent about it any longer. I've noticed, over the years, there's been three or four particularly outspoken patients who've been critical of you, and have ended up being severely brain-damaged after being administered ECT. I've noticed that the deeply depressed patients who aren't critical of you at all, the ones who are nice and compliant, just the way you like them, are given ECT and usually just come out with mild memory loss. Nowhere near as severe as the ones who dare to criticise you, eh?'

'You're sounding more and more like one of my delusional patients by the moment,' he retorts breezily, shaking his head and tutting. 'It's funny you know - it always seems to be the delusional ones who fancy themselves to be really perceptive.'

'At first I was even in favour of giving ECT to some of those patients myself,' I say, ignoring his implied threat, 'because I was finding it heart-wrenching to listen to their testimonies of what had happened to them, and I figured that if ECT does result in memory loss, then erasing some of those traumatic memories could help to reduce their suffering. But now I know the memories are necessary, so that people are able to understand the context of their suffering and explore the personal meanings that can be drawn from that. Erasing memories has the effect of concealing the actions of the perpetrators of abuse, and is therefore complicit with those injustices.'

'Angelina, what you need to understand is that sometimes patients' brains malfunction so seriously when they have major depressive disorder, and become so deeply depressed, that ECT is a necessary means of jolting them out of it. And you'll remember that you're the one who's been reporting to me that Adele's been showing signs of deep depression ever since she got here.'

I'm prickling with renewed anger now, because it feels like he's implying I'm complicit with what's happened to Adele.

'No, no, don't you dare try to put this on me!' I say, lowering my voice to something like a controlled hiss. 'And by the way, I'm well aware you're supposed to give these people numerous options and alternatives in terms of treatments and interventions, before trying something as drastic as ECT. And I'm certain you haven't been doing that.'

'You're quite the know it all, it would seem, aren't you Angelina,' he comments breezily, 'which is funny because you really know precious little.'

'Oh really?' I fire back at him. 'I reckon you'd be quite disconcerted by what I know actually, doctor. I know exactly what's going on here. Adele was becoming very outspoken on the ward, wasn't she? Criticising the diagnosis of major depressive disorder you've given her. You didn't like that at all, did you? She was telling the other patients your assertion that she's suffering from a malfunctioning brain or brain disease is nonsense, and she was adamant that, on the contrary, her distress has been an understandable reaction to mistreatment at the hands of her husband and the circumstances of her life. She was telling the patients that you never even asked about how her experiences contributed to her distress, and some patients revealed that they hadn't been asked either. So she lit the touch paper there, so to speak, didn't she, eh? She questioned the whole idea of whether people's emotional distress should be seen as a medical issue at all. She exposed the way psychiatry pathologises and decontextualises people's distress, by locating it as a flaw within the brain and biology of the individual, but she championed the argument that people's emotional distress is intelligible in terms of the context and circumstances of their lives, which threatens to undermine not just your own authority, doctor, but the very legitimacy of psychiatry itself, and by extension, the huge profits made by pharmaceutical companies who manufacture pills for the countless numbers of psychiatric brain diseases that've been fabricated over the years. Of course, every profession that there has ever been will tend to do what is necessary to sustain itself. So, doctor, you administered a dangerously large dose of ECT to Adele with the intention of causing severe brain damage, as a result of which her memory of the abuse she suffered at the hands of her husband is now lost, and her ability to be articulate and eloquent is also lost, meaning that she can no longer champion her cause and threaten the validity of psychiatry. In short, doctor, you've brain-damaged her to rip away her voice and silence her.'

Dr Harpoon claps mockingly. 'You fancy yourself as quite the detective don't you, Angelina?' he sneers. 'I'm sure I can't remember ever hearing such a far-fetched story. For a start, you'll have a hell of a job getting any doctor, surgeon or psychiatrist to substantiate your wacky claim that Adele's been brain-damaged. The more you do that, the more you'll highlight the way Adele's behaving in a very peculiar, attention-seeking and manipulative way, and therefore render her ever more likely to receive a secondary diagnosis with a personality disorder, comprendez?' He leans towards me again and smiles slyly. 'Or maybe, you'll just end up drawing attention to how she's been experimenting dangerously with recreational drugs?'

'Stop it, stop it!' I say, my voice shaking with emotion. 'I'll find a way of exposing you, Dr Harpoon. You may have silenced Adele, but I'll be her voice from now on. And If I can't get you on grounds of intention to cause brain damage, I'll find another way of getting you. For one thing, I know that you haven't been securing proper, valid consent to carry out ECT on the patients. Patients need to have access to sufficient information about the benefits and risks of the proposed treatment and any alternative treatments before they can decide to give consent. I happen to know that you've only been informing them about the benefits, to give a false impression of its effectiveness, which means you haven't been giving a balanced amount of information that they reasonably need to make their decision, so their consent can't be valid.'

Dr Harpoon draws in a deep breath and brings his interlocked fingers carefully to rest on the desk in front of him.

'Angelina, while I do have some admiration for your misguided zeal, I have to ask you to stop for a moment and think about the way things are. I'll humour you for a moment and entertain the possibility that adverse experiences and events are the true underlying causes of people's psychological distress. Nevertheless, there are huge vested interests in pathologising and decontextualising people's distress, as you insist on putting it, and locating the flaw within the brain and biological makeup of the individual, because it gives politicians and those in power the perfect excuse to do nothing about the social and economic problems that are supposedly underlying people's emotional distress. Tackling those vast problems would be a huge undertaking, and one that they'd prefer to turn a blind eye to, quite frankly. That's why the disease model of emotional distress will endure.'

'But if the disease model of emotional distress is really as stubbornly entrenched as you make it out to be, why would you feel the need to silence Adele?' I ask, casting him a quizzical look. 'Maybe the legitimacy of the disease model is more vulnerable to attack than you care to admit. Using ECT to commit an atrocity smacks of being the desperate measure of a sham pseudo-science that is all too painfully aware of the gathering voices who are threatening its conceptual fragility. I'm gonna make damn sure there's a parliamentary enquiry into this.'

Adele

My heart's beating very fast. One of the nurses just told me that my husband's here to visit me! All I can remember is his name. Ralph. Yes, I'm sure it's Ralph. Be a bit embarrassing if I've got it wrong. Hope not. I can't even remember what he looks like, or much else about him, if I'm honest.

Still, I'm feeling very excited, almost like a flustered teenager.

I sit at a table in the dining area, waiting for him.

A man enters the room and walks over to me.

'Hello Adele,' he says. He's got a nice smile and I'm glad to say he's not bad looking at all.

'Hello...Ralph?' I say hesitantly.

'May I?' he asks, pointing at the seat opposite mine.

'Yeah...yes.'

He sits himself down, takes a deep breath, and his face breaks out into a broad grin. I find myself smiling back, feeling like a bit of a fool.

Neither of us say anything. We just gaze at one another.

He's rubbing his forefinger and thumb together, I notice. Maybe he's nervous or something. Reminds me a bit of a housefly, if I'm honest.

THE END

A message from the author....connect with James Field

If you enjoyed **Groatcrest**, it would be great if you could consider leaving a short review on Amazon to help others discover it (or favourite me!) at https://www.amazon.com/-/e/B01KCX2ZHK I'm curious to know your thoughts and I'd love for you to get in touch. Honest reader reviews help others decide whether they'll enjoy a book. If you believe your friends will like my book, do let them know. Follow me on Twitter at https://twitter.com/Convivial55

Thank you!

James Field

Here are my other works of literary fiction, all of which are available at: https://www.amazon.com/-/e/B01KCX2ZHK

-The Gaslighteur

-Self-aware Sonic

-Personalisation Order

-The Noble Trick

www.ingramcontent.com/pod-product-compliance
Lightning Source LLC
Chambersburg PA
CBHW070653130626
46555CB00006B/2859